Wrinkles and Cloudy Days

George Paraschiv

Illustrated by

Maria Tabarcea

Dobroești
2023

Hardcover ISBN: 978-973-0-38255-6

For information, contact the publisher at georgeparaschiv8@yahoo.com

Visit the author's website at www.georgeparaschiv.com

Illustration and design by Maria Tabarcea

First Edition

TO MY PARENTS

CONTENTS

BOTANICS

NOVEMBER RAIN

The rain hit the windshield like small hammers with a big plan. The wipers were too old to fight the weather, the rubber on them too squeaky. Felt more like it was hurting the glass, scratching it, so they were long turned off, right after the car had been neatly parked. The radio was on, news o'clock, but you couldn't really understand what the reporter was saying and Albert didn't really care for the volume button. He was too busy with his thoughts, too focused on staying focused, every minute checking the view through the passenger's seat window. He slowly and softly tapped his index finger on the wheel. It didn't really match the rhythm of his feelings, but his arthritis wouldn't let him speed up the tempo. Albert kept the engine on his old sedan turned on, something he didn't usually do, given his self-sufficient, economic character. But this time it was different. He wanted to keep the car warm. This time he was waiting for his son.

He remembered a time some 30 years before. It was autumn, but warmer than this one, without such dreadful rain. The trees were a gorgeous reddish colour and their falling leaves were the only reason he'd sometimes use the not yet squeaky wipers. Standing outside his car, he'd look around this new carpet covering the concrete to pick the most beautiful maple tree leaf, loving to help his young son's collection of perfectly symmetrical autumn leaves. Other parents would greet him and he'd reply, sometimes even making small talk about the kids' grades and homework, all while searching for that perfect leaf. Then he'd hear the school bell and in a couple of minutes his son, Leonard, would come out excited and smiling with only one thing on his mind.

"Dad, did you find any?!"

He always did and some were good and some were not really what his son was looking for.

"We'll stop on our way home to look for more, alright champ?"

"Awesome!" Leo would shout. "I'm gonna be the world's greatest botanist!"

He looked through the window again and the gates were opening. He couldn't really tell right away, but his son was there, coming out, getting wet by the unforgiving rain. Albert jump-started his old body, grabbed the umbrella from his back seat, got out of the car and crossed the street in a hurry, trying to get his son cover from the rain. They didn't say "Hello", not formally at least, but they both got under the old umbrella, or so was the plan. It was too small for both of them so Albert walked mostly outside of it, leaning his head under it, holding it over his son as they rushed towards the car.

Inside they patted their clothes to shoo the extra water. Albert might have done it for a bit too long, maybe trying to avoid the interaction. But with their clothes all dried up, the closed umbrella lying in the backseat, the silence was growing more tense, demanding something more.

"How are you, Leonard?"

His wife was better at ice breaking, tending to awkward and tense situations, better with words, just better with people, but she wasn't around anymore. He could've gone the cowardly way, turning on the ignition and simply driving away, shoving all this tension under the rug of their relationship. But he wasn't getting any younger and he sure as hell wasn't gonna let feelings from the past outlive him.

"I'm good, pops. Glad to be out" Leonard replied. He even made a bit of eye contact. Even cracked a smile for a split second. Made things easier for Albert.

It was theft. It was his view of the world. It was the wrong crowd at the right time in his teenage years. It was his father's unforeseen change to an underpaid job, working overtime, when Leonard was twelve. It was bad fortune playing with a family's principles. Albert knew. He blamed his son when he first heard about it. He blamed him for breaking his mother's heart. But deep inside he knew. So through the mist of disappointment, he blamed himself. For not being there all the time. Not enough father-son moments. Not enough beers on their porch discussing life's values. Not kicking the ball enough times. Not being smart enough to get a better job, so he could find the perfect leaf with his son.

It was a long night for Albert.

"That damn rain…" he muffled in his pillow. But then again, the past few years all nights were long. The rain actually kind of helped, taking his mind off of things.

Might as well get a glass of milk, or an excuse to wonder around the house at two in the morning. He was going to the kitchen, but along the way he noticed the cracked door to the balcony. His son was sitting there, smoking a cigarette, looking at the rain. Albert didn't know what to do. He stumbled with leaving him alone and the fatherly approach of maybe talking to him.

"I'm alright, pops. Go to bed" Leonard calmly solved his father's dilemma without even turning.

Albert muttered something about just getting a glass of milk, then staggered across the kitchen and back to his bedroom. There was uncertainty, regret and fear all combined into one corrosive feeling. It couldn't have ended with his son's release day, because he knew these things don't magically get solved that way. These places don't make you a better person than when you go in. Quite often, it's the contrary and this scared him. He didn't know what would come next, but luckily, or some might say unfortunately, he grabbed on to a light branch of hope. Not for his own life to change, because he was an old man and time wasn't on his side, but for his son's. Maybe he could go for the smallest things that might help keep his son off the wrong path. Maybe a word here, a word there or just any show of support. He settled on this and it helped more than the milk.

The next morning came just like most did these days; a bit too soon, while it was still dark. He'd usually go out on the balcony and watch the sky getting brighter, over a glass of water and some bread to feed the pigeons that would visit him. Things were different today. He thought of finding his son still there, on the balcony, still smoking, still watching the rain. Or maybe just a full ashtray, demanding to be cleaned. Or the imagined clogged air reminding him of how much he hated cigarettes and just vices in general. But his surprise overwhelmed his relief as there was no ashtray, no clogged air, no rain and no son. Matter of fact, his son was nowhere in sight, nowhere in the house. Default thoughts settled on Albert's mind. Runaway, trouble coping, return to the bad stuff. He feared he didn't even get a chance to try his plan. A word here, a word there, it would never have worked.

Maybe it was too soon. Maybe he just went for a walk.

Around noon, there he was. Back home, with a bag full of stuff and a simple line for his father.

"Hope you read my note, pops. Left it on the coffee table."

Albert was caught off-guard, but his ego helped him recover quickly.

"I don't drink coffee anymore" he replied as he suspiciously focused on his recently released son's bag.

"Uhum… I'll be in the bedroom."

The rest of the day past with a couple more superficial interactions and the night just like before. A glass of milk, a cracked door, a smoking cigarette and that dreadful rain again. And so did the next few days. And then the rain stopped.

Albert woke up a bit later that day. The rain must have finally caught up with him and although he couldn't admit it to himself, staying in bed past eight o'clock actually helped his body and his mood. Moving around the house, he anticipated another awkward interaction with his son. He realized he was just as guilty, if not even more, for the awkwardness, but couldn't get himself to follow through with his own plan. Today, even if he tried, it would have been a bit more difficult. His son, again, wasn't at home.

"Quite a few busy… hectic… days for a recently released man" he thought. He couldn't help judging, but he stopped and regretted doing so, most times. Then again what would a recently released man do inside? You'd figure he would've had more than enough time to sit and contemplate. Albert did this daily ever since he found out his son was going to go to prison. A rigid man in his thinking, he battled his thoughts, he battled his principles, his beliefs, to open his mind, to make room for new perspectives, for a new attitude. For forgiveness. He struggled.

He went about his regular, non-rainy day routine that had been postponed for the last week. A short walk to the nearby park, a place where he and his wife would sometimes spend their afternoons, followed by a trip to the local grocery store for some fresh fruits. Along the way he'd usually meet some acquaintances and make a bit of small talk. Today however, he feared there'd be no small talk because these people knew his situation and they would certainly ask about his son's release.

He wasn't going to avoid it though. He'd endure it and get it over with. And so he went. And so they asked. It wasn't so bad.

"People are just trying to be nice" he realized, having a front row ticket on his own emotional rollercoaster. The day went by easier than he thought.

With a small bag of apples and apricots, Albert approached his house. He was surprised to see Leonard on the porch, looking like he was waiting for someone. Even more surprised that he was wearing a shirt and a tie. He couldn't remember when had been the last time he saw him dressed like this. Probably high school.

"How you doin', pops?"

"Good. I'm good… Got some apples." He opened his bag to sort of prove it. "You want some? I handpicked them myself" he softly said as he handed one to his son.

Leonard chuckled. "Sure" he replied.

"Good. They're good for you" Albert said as he went on inside the house. One hand in his pocket, another holding that shinny Granny Smith apple, Leonard checked his shoes for no reason, took a deep breath and followed his dad inside.

"Listen, pops, I wanna tell you something."

Albert put the apples in a bowl and, after he took his time, replied.

"Go ahead."

"I got a job" Leonard confessed. Like he did something wrong. Again. "It ain't much" and he broke eye contact. "Just a cashier at that big supermarket down the ring road. But I thought you should know." He connected eyes again, this time with some fresh confidence.

Albert had hoped to hear something like this since he saw that nicely ironed shirt and the well executed tie knot.

"I'm glad to hear that. That's good. It's a good thing" refraining his full sentiments from showing. Life had been harsh on him so now he was taking it one step at a time, cautious, not forcing this turn for the better. Just being there for his son should be enough.

All of his life's weight had been on this three legged chair, hoping for better days or at least a start from scratch. It looked like a start from scratch now. With this news, for the first time, it seemed his struggle had not been in vain.

More days and morning and nights and weeks past. The awkward interactions were less and less and replaced with longer and longer talks about work, about life, about Leonard's mother and Albert's wife, about the past and after a certain point, even about prison and regret, even about judgement and forgiveness. It went both ways. After a while, their duo talks welcomed a third person, as Leonard met someone. Albert liked her and he actually couldn't believe it would all turn out alright after just about a year. He almost felt lucky or blessed. "It's just finally balancing out..." he thought. His part in all of this was done and he wished his wife, from up there in heaven, would see how things eventually came to be.

One day he spent a bit more time on the balcony, feeding the pigeons, breathing the fresh air, but this time watching the daylight fade away. He went to bed and didn't need any milk to fall asleep. Things were alright.

LIVING ROOM PIANO

It sounded like piano music and it was coming from my living room. I almost forgot the thing was even there. Dusting is the only time we intersect nowadays. But the sweet notes caressed the water I was bringing from the kitchen, tiny concentrical waves dancing inside these glasses. Felt like they were celebrating meeting each-other on a tray again as I usually only use one at a time. I don't get visitors all that often now. As I approached the living room I was even more surprised to see that it wasn't Peter or his lovely wife, Joan, that were playing the piano, but their youngest, Daniel. Of course, children do play the piano, but not in such a mature way. My otherwise lonely home was now filled with lively emotion, like taking back the years, resurfacing feelings I forgot were there.

I didn't say a word. Didn't even enter the room. Didn't want to disturb the music. There was no place for my squeaky floor to accompany such a rare occurrence. I looked at his parents sitting on the sofa and they smiled at me, none of us undergoing any sudden movements, like observing a rare animal in the wild, respecting its beauty and hoping our presence didn't ruin the moment. We were supposed to be silent, but their smile was as loud as the music. My smile on the other hand, slowly emerging, was fragile, struggling not to appear intimidated by this prodigious music the kid was playing. Such music is a gift, but the playing was what baffled me the most. How could one live such few years, yet forward feelings you get to know in a lifetime? You can play the notes, but I'm sure you can't transmit the feeling without feeling it yourself. The piece ended.

"Should I play another?" the young boy asked his father.

They laughed at his stoic response. I laughed too. How could you not? Contrast creates humor and there was great contrast between such a simple and respectful question and the unleashed poetic manipulation of that dusty keyboard just a few seconds before.

“Ask Mr. David here. It’s his piano” his father answered as he passed this weight to me. How could I ever get in the way of such art filling my living room again. It’d be against all that’s good in the world.

“Of course. Certainly!” I rushed my slow starting words, still baffled by what was happening. I rushed my feet too, like running late for opening night at the movies, crouching a bit to not let my silhouette disturb the other privileged people around me. “Just let me put these on the coffee table, so I can sit down and listen more carefully to your playing.”

I then slowly sat in my armchair, letting all that worn cushion embrace me to its exhaustion, making sure my position wouldn’t need readjusting after the playing started. I gave a small nod to his father, received a smile in return and he let his child know he could now go for it. And then it started again.

The emotion. It was still there. I wasn’t wrong the first time, though for the few seconds while I placed those glasses on the coffee table I doubted my judgement. Maybe it was just me getting rusty, not really listening to piano music since Marie died, maybe I had craved it, settling now for just any playing, my instincts fooling me. But now I was sure. The emotion was authentic. It still filled the room. It still thrilled my soul. It still looked at me as I looked for it around the room. The boy played a beautiful melancholic piece, not much different from the first one. I knew both of them. They where the creation of a not so famous, yet remarkable, contemporary German composer, Axel Ritter, an old man by now, about 10 years my junior. With all the emotions raveling through the room at that point, I wasn’t surprised by the musical pick. I knew the boy’s father, Peter, my ex student at the College of Arts, was fascinated by German art, most of his college essays I reviewed revolving around German subjects. But Mr. Ritter’s work had been hijacked. The young boy played the songs like he himself wrote them half an hour before, meaning every single push of a key. He played them raw, making them his own, yet still letting this hidden mature soul drip on the keyboard.

This wasn’t the first time parents brought their offspring to me for my specialized “eye for talent”, given my art analyst background and my involvement in cultural projects. I had a good reputation as an arts professor. My students liked me, and more importantly, they trusted my opinion.

Though I'd tell quite instantly if the youngster is truly gifted or just at the beginning of a long road towards developing a regular career, I'd give a good listen to their violin playing, I'd follow every dried brush stroke on their painting, I'd weigh every word in their prose and then I'd guide them and their parents towards a certain tutor or professor to sharpen their skill. Most of them were closer to their teenage years though. I'm sure the last one is far from being a rookie in his career by now. It had been a while. But what a way for this undeciphered talent to find me, especially in the form of piano playing, my wife's profession. Maybe it's her way of thawing the piano strings. Maybe she sent her talent and feelings to touch this dusty piano once more. Maybe I just miss her.

I usually applauded the young person in front of me, no matter their degree of talent, as encouragement. No matter the lack of talent, I always believed, and it was proven to me many times, that hard work can more than make up for it. So encouraging them seemed the right thing to do. Not this time.

The second piece ended and I was struggling to come to grips with reality, I was rearranging my feelings as I tried to keep a solid face. It was art in its purest form. Art should make people feel. And it should also be original. And it was. An original take on those two German pieces. My silence was a bit too tense.

"Mr. David. What did you think?" asked his father. Unlike most other similar questions addressed to me in the past by hopeful parents, this one didn't carry any nervousness, any wish for a positive response. Peter knew all too well how special his son was. Still, his courtesy was well intended, just as I remember him.

I looked at him and his wife and I smiled.

"You have a very, very talented son. I am very happy for you two and for the young boy." I needn't say more. One could've thought the years had taken their toll and I had became less strict, less demanding or just simply old. Like a car tyre becomes old and looses its grip. Old like a wooden chair you don't trust with your weight anymore. Old not like wine, but like a bottle of water out in the sun. You'd never wash your eyes with that water.

But the boy's talent was obvious. His performance was sublime. Analyzing his technique, his delivery, his phrasing would've been a waste of energy and an insult to ourselves. We should just enjoy the feeling.

I was, however, still intrigued.

I leaned towards the boy. “Young man… I’m sure you listen to a lot of Mr. Axel Ritter’s work back home” I looked for a second at his father and he subtly giggled. “And I’m sure he’d be very happy to know his compositions are played so beautifully by the hands of a newer generation. But what I’m curious about is what do you think of when you play these songs, when you play the piano…”

I didn’t want to put too much weight on this question. There’s only so much a 7 year old can tell you about how his mind works.

“I don’t think about anything” the boy replied.

“Yes. That is true in a way. Then what do you feel, or better yet, what does it feel like when you play the piano?” I was hopeful.

His eyes drew towards the ceiling, an indication he was trying to remember, he was being truthful. “Well… maybe the purple flowers.”

“The purple flowers?” I asked. Peter and Joan seemed as puzzled as me this time.

“Yes. The purple flowers. Like the ones where we get bread” he looked at his parents for help with the explanation.

“Daniel, do you mean the bakery?” his mother asked. “Where Mrs. Cheryl works? The lady that gives you a free pretzel?”

Daniel nodded.

“And the purple flowers?” she continued.

“There were purple flowers on the table. That day, when you talked a lot to her.”

Joan thought for a second. Peter had no clue what this was about.

“The lavender? The purple flowers with the strong smell?” she asked.

Daniel nodded again.

“She sometimes puts lavender on the counter. I think she grows it at home and brings it to her bakery” she explained it to me. “She’s a lovely lady, but she has been going through some rough time since her husband divorced her…”

“That’s why we stayed a lot that day. You talked a lot to her” Daniel added.

We stared at each-other, all of us, for a few seconds, then I gathered some words, then I took it upon myself to further my curiosity.

Bakery
1,00
4,00
5,00
4,00
0,50
3,00

19.00

"So Daniel, you think of the lavender… the purple flowers when you play the piano?"

"Well, not all the songs" he corrected me.

"Right, not all. But at least these two."

"I think so."

It couldn't have been just empathy. A child could never understand an adult's troubles, the complexity of being heartbroken, the many ways stress wraps around our minds, let alone from hearing a single conversation. But the piano playing showed otherwise.

I turned to his parents. "If he really has the ability to capture such sentiments just from seeing them in others… then that is a true gift. The fact that he has the capacity to release such captured sentiments in a flawless way through the strings of a piano is immense. Empathy is what makes us better humans… I think. And this is so much more than empathy…"

I guess we were happy, just still baffled by what we discovered, so we just sat there, not really saying a word, processing all the opportunities the boy now had, the responsibilities and the consequences of such a gift, all the power. However, for a moment it almost slipped my mind, the more important aspect of all of this…

"So Daniel… do you love playing piano?"

"Yeah. I like it" he answered.

"Alright. You like it. But do you love it? Like you'd love a pet dog?"

He thought for a second.

"Mmm… yes, sir. I love it."

I smiled. It kind of took that weight of his shoulders. And it was a heavy gift.

"But I really, really love drawing" he added.

*

It was hard to believe he'd be just as talented at drawing as he was in playing the piano. And he wasn't. A week later, his dad dropped by again to bring some of his drawings. He knew.

I recommended a tutor, an old colleague of mine, a very talented artist that inspired many young people to pursue a career in visual arts. I pitied his parents for having to deal with such a decision. I pitied the world of humanity for being on the brink of losing such art. But selfishness isn't always bad. I'd say looking at the view for yourself, taking it all in, is way ahead of photographing it. You can always photograph it later. Or draw it… I guess that's what Daniel would do.

WRINKLES

He ran his finger down and up over his eye wrinkles, continuously, like not believing it. Repeatedly, like denying it. His sunglasses hid this growing complex. He wore them even on a cloudy day like this. "The Italians wear glasses even on a cloudy day" a friend told him ten years ago, long before his skin sketched those wrinkles, yet fashion would've been too shallow of a reason to do this back then. He had his practical reason now, but it came with the bitter taste of witnessing growing old.

The waiter dribbled the other seated customers to reach Paul's favorite table hidden in the corner of this lovely garden terrace. He sat, legs crossed,to the left of the table, the chair not facing it, leaning one elbow over the smooth white cotton table cloth and holding a small coffee cup over his upper leg with his other hand. It was like he was having lunch with that table. Truc colleagues, ready for a midday gossip.

"Blueberry muffin, sir?" the waiter smugly raced his words ahead of Paul's.

A defeated grin welcomed the young waiter's proposal.

"That's right. How'd you know? You're new around here" Paul asked intrigued.

"I am new, sir. But Martin told me you are not. He told me about your blueberry muffin. I also know about the Friday strawberry pancake with extra maple sirup."

"Is that so? I'm not surprised with Martin's managerial skills. He's always been very dedicated to his profession. However, hearing it from you now, I must seem quite a pretentious guest" Paul thoughtfully confessed.

"The blueberry muffin is not to be missed during the week, sir. And what a better way to celebrate the coming of the weekend than with a rich pancake" the new waiter said with an almost soldier-like attitude.
The warm smile gave away his civilian status and his future as Martin's successor.

"Truer words have never been spoken. Thank you."

*

Paul was a regular. He built this status over the years. The smooth skin around his eyes witnessed it.

Some people were seen there quite often, but not as often as Paul, others were new, just visitors stoping for a quick cup of coffee, just strangers. Like the young couple sitting three tables away from Paul, sipping on their lemonades and ignoring the complementary olives the young waiter brought them. Too green to relish delicate aromas. The olives, however, were perfectly ripe, one of the products this lovely place took great pride in, thus serving them for free to everyone. Well, almost to everyone. The old lady sitting at the table in the center of the terrace always insisted on paying for them, explaining how she feels morally obligated to disburse for such spectacular fruits, her sharp and short laughter admitting it's just a quirky way of tipping the waiter. But it wasn't just the guests or the ever gracious staff that defined this place, and however delicious the food was or however perfectly hot the coffee cup that warmed his hand was, there was something else that made this place special for Paul. Most of the other regulars thought he worked or lived nearby as they always saw him here, but some of the staff members knew Paul lived way across town and he did freelance work as an interior designer, so location was far from a reason. Maybe it was the smooth sound the waterfall statues made accompanied by the music of some birds he never knew the name of that soothed his mind, the perfect lunch break to kickstart his work mindset.

"Or maybe his mistress lives nearby" the old lady thought. But Paul wasn't married, so maybe his supposed mistress was just his future wife. The people that wondered about him were probably more sure than he was.

*

The day's lunch ritual was almost over. There's only so much time you can spend with a lonely table and its beautiful white cloth, so Paul let the young waiter know that he's done. Normally, people would ask for a check, some people mastering a smooth hand gesture, an artistic signature on the paperless air in front of them and taking a weird pride after getting the confirmation from the waiter, but Paul was long past this phase. Having the same things everyday, even the most distracted businessman would eventually memorize the price, so there's no need for a check to be brought and there's no need for fancy hand language. The money, including a respectful tip, left under his coffee cup so that the wind won't steal it and a courteous nod accompanied by a smiley "goodbye" as he himself dribbled the other tables were enough.

He stopped for a minute right outside the wrought metal gates of the terrace to turn his phone back on as he always shut it down when having lunch, and as he tidied his raincoat he lifted his eyes like someone called for their gaze. No-one really did. But someone was there, on the other side of the road, window shopping at a small home decoration store. He couldn't see her face, but that long straight chestnut hair made him instantly hope it's someone he once knew. Long before the wrinkles.

There was a cross walk about fifty meters away and although his curiosity rushed him to jaywalk over this narrow and, quite frankly, unofficially pedestrian road, he chose to take his time. It was going to take him two minutes to get to her, but it felt like twenty as she could have left for the opposite direction and he didn't want to creepily approach her from behind, another reason he didn't want to jaywalk straight to her. Yet with each approaching step, she was still there in front of that window, looking quite immersed in the act of choosing new stuff for her house, making Paul feel lucky to synchronize just as his spontaneous plan outlined.

*

"Carmen?" he confidently said. Feelings, whether melancholy, insecurity or fear, were just for him. For others, there was only the right attitude. A person is what he does, not what he thinks. He thought.

"Heey!" she lingered her greeting after a few silent seconds reading their past in his eyes. It was going to be the last time she'd "mention" it in this conversation.

"I kinda like the sky-patterned pillows. Makes one forget about these cloudy days" he profoundly said.

"I thought you loved the rain. And autumn" she slyly replied to his goofy comment.

Another few silent seconds.

"I do. You got me" he surrendered.

They both laughed. They hugged.

"How have you been, Paul?" she promptly took the lead.

"I'm good. Secretly enjoying the clouded day and telling strangers I bump into otherwise" he said and smiled.

She laughed. "But I'm not a stranger, am I?" sarcastically changing her tone.

He smiled. "No. I guess you could never be."

She looked away. Almost blushed. The type of situation one would usually consider going in a "right" direction. Paul was cautious though. They had history, the type of history that ended well, a long time ago, before wrinkles, weekly menus, and the ability to leave a nice tip. The type of history one doesn't want to ruin by letting a lost butterfly rebel against mature reason. And how come she wasn't trying on the vintage jackets at the boutique next door. Or drooling over the gourmet eclairs at that lovely french pastry shop. You could smell the vanilla from across the street. A home decoration store screams a life already planned. A family.

Welcome

“I have to be somewhere in about an hour, so I was gonna kill some time. I know a nice place around here. They have good tea.” He slowed down his sentences. “Maybe I’ll get some tea. Do you wanna get some tea with me? a smile emerging as he sketched that question mark.

She smiled as well, dropping her eyes, jumping ahead to conclusions, though she didn’t really have any reason to be overcautious. They knew each other too well to play games, plus they were past that age. Being adults saves a lot of time. Meeting with an old friend for tea is what adults do.

“I guess I have some spare time myself ” she happily said.

But Carmen was indeed playing a game. Not the superficial conscious flirting game of a teenager trying to juggle hard-to-get with smooth reeling in, but the subconscious game of analyzing the situation and not rushing into it and showing the person standing in front of her all of this process, even if it’s only through the descent of her look and the short pause before her answer. It said enough about her for the moment. And he loved it.

*

Old buildings slimming down the light that hit these narrow streets, narrowed even more by the chairs of small cafés or the occasional wooden sign of a family owned shop, smooth sidewalks polished by millions of feet from different centuries, all of this caressed by the music of buskers every other corner. The streets in this part of town had a subtle flow that kept pedestrians at a balanced pace, making their trip unnoticeable, enjoyable, encouraging their chat dynamic. A perfect environment for old friends to revisit memories, to revisit who they were that long ago, but Paul and Carmen didn’t jump into their older selves right away, out of respect for each other’s present self. People change and after so much time it’s like meeting someone new. You don’t just ask new people to turn into someone you want, no matter if you think you’ve met them in a different life. You helplessly hope they will.

Still their walk was far from awkward, mainly because of their chemistry, something those sky-patterned pillows witnessed right from the beginning.

"God, I love this part of town" Carmen said.

"Yeah… and it only gets better with time" he added.

"Didn't you miss it while you were gone?" She almost regretted right away asking this question.

"I did" he boldly answered. "Still sort of missing it. Maybe the way it was back then, you know?" he raised his eyes from his walking feet. "More like regretting missing those years" he eventually confessed and dropped his eyes back to the smooth pavement.

"Well, it must not have been easy anyway…" she tried to empathize.

"Yeah, well after what happened with my mother, I kinda needed to get away for a while. Dad didn't really seem to miss me, so I didn't rush to get back." He abruptly stoped talking, like analyzing the situation for the first time in his mind. "You should see us now. Best of friends. Took us only 13 years apart to get to that" he said laughing lightly.

Carmen smiled and laughed too. "Where did you go? I heard something about Norway."

"Yes. Norway for a while. A bit cold. I needed that. Then I moved to Madrid for college. Didn't finish it at first. Plenty of distractions. Went to Moscow. Lived there with some friends for a couple of years. Came back to Madrid. Finished college, got my degree, and then just jumped around Europe for work. It was good experience I guess" he said nodding, pleased with his memories.

"That sounds really exciting. So you speak Russian, right?" she asked.

Paul laughed. "You'd think so, I know. Fortunately, my French is so much better, perfect for this lovely café right here" he said as he stoped.

"Oh, I know this place. Pretty cozy. Good tea indeed."

"True, now let's not ruin it by talking anymore about me and my Russian skills" he said as they both started laughing.

*

The chat went on, balanced more towards her life's story. She told him about college, work, trips and different experiences, failed relationships and life lessons. Paul realized it wasn't the different distant countries that separated him from the ones back home, but the many, many years. Time is more vicious than distance. Someone recently told him the same thing. Maybe it was the wrinkles.

Word by word, they were getting there, letting their guard down, remembering who they were back then, discovering a type of time travel. Nothing too free, as their present personalities were judging from the shadows of their mind, but enough to wake up some dusty feelings.

No matter how good their chemistry was, a good laugh can sometimes end on a melancholic note, leaving a long pause up for the grabs.

His smile lingered still on his face. "That's a nice store" he said. "Where we met today. A lot of great stuff for your house."

"Yes. I know. But I've never really bought anything. I was probably going to today, yet… this… stopped me." She laughed.

She didn't mention a current boyfriend or a husband in their chat. This intrigued Paul.

"I'd say that I'd like to do this again." He hesitated a bit and she sensed it, so she didn't intervene. "And although you didn't mention it, I'm thinking a great person like you can't be single. Still, I'm hoping that you are. I also hope the only thing you were searching in that shop was a photo frame for your dog."

It took some courage to say this. Last time he sought the same amount of courage he was 15 and it was for a simple "Hi". To the same girl.

She took a deep breath. "I'm sorry, but… I don't have a dog" she said with a professional poker face. She broke the three most confusing seconds of their meeting with a slow emerging smile. He smiled as well. Laughed. It was all clear.

Second tip of the day and they were off for another walk through the same lovely streets, continuing their nice chat, something it seems they've waited for some time. He walked her to her car and they just lingered one more minute. "Funny how things happen" they both thought.

"Never thought of sky-patterned pillows as a relationship symbol?" she said ironically.

"You'd never believe it, I know. Deal breaker" he responded.
They laughed.

"Good tea. Really liked it. I'm glad we met. Again" Carmen said.

"Me too. Glad you liked the good tea."

"I can drop you off somewhere if you want" she offered.

"I'm fine, thanks! My car is parked across the street, next to "Pane e Vino".

"Is that the place your mom used to take you for ice cream when you were a kid? Carmen asked.

"Did I tell you about that?" Paul asked surprised.

"Yes. Back in the day, when you got tipsy all you talked about was her."

"Now when I get tipsy all I talk about is you" he said closing in on her, goofily.

"Stop it" and she jokingly slapped his shoulder.

"Yeah, I guess that's the place."

"Do you go there often?" she said on a more serious note. He took a second before answering.

"Not really..."

Feelings were just for him. At least some.

DO I KNOW YOU?

Over a hundred years of aviation and I still had to stop in Prague for three hours to get from Oslo to Lisbon. I expected three hours of reading a book and maybe eating one of the local goulash soups with a puffy pretzel on the side. Never really liked airports. A bit too crowded for me, too much chaos. So different from our house at the edge of the woods, a place only crowded by the trees. But I wasn't flying for work, which made it more tolerable. I'd been taking this trip for the last 5 years now, just not alone, but with my wife, who this time couldn't come because of complications with a work project. We visit our daughter every autumn in Portugal ever since she moved there. She married there and I like to joke with her husband that I only stand him because of the opportunity to experience a warm autumn every year. He's a good kid and I like his whole family. They're warmer beyond what the sun could do to Portugal.

After following what I could only describe as too many signs, I exited the maze of corridors in the Prague airport to arrive in the main waiting area, relatively close to my next gate. I window shopped a bit, thinking this would consume my waiting time, then I looked for "the perfect" seat, something overly ambitious and pretentious as most of them were already taken.

I did find something good enough, though, so I sat down. A few texts with my wife, told her I loved her and that I was sorry she'd have to endure a ton of Facebook photos of me in the pool while she's working in a freezing country, and then I opened my book. My reading turned more into shuffling the pages. I couldn't really concentrate. Maybe I was excited. Maybe I was bored. There was a new bar in the middle of this waiting area or maybe last year's book was more interesting and I didn't notice it. A nice Irish bar, or pub as they call it, shaped like a horse shoe where people sat like knights at a huge round table, if the round table was cut in half, had bar stools and two bartenders in the middle.

It had suspended TV sets showing the game and I could hear some nice music, different from the ambient airport music. It also served food, and although it also had small tables around it, it seemed all places were taken. Part of me didn't want to risk losing my precious seat just to hover around the bar until a place freed up, though the game and a refreshing gin and tonic to celebrate my upcoming vacation just couldn't wait. So I hovered indeed, but not for long, as a young gentleman bottomed up his beer to run for boarding. Just as fast, I claimed the newly freed seat among the privileged others. Lucky, glad and squeezed between loud tipsy people and their travel bags, I just couldn't wait for my gin and tonic. One of the bartenders, a lady about 10 years my senior, helped me right away. She looked like the other bartender's superior, still she did most of the work. She sang while doing beer refills, but she didn't know all the lyrics, so she mostly mumbled or hummed. She seemed to enjoy her job. And then I saw it.

Among the bunch of people discussing, laughing, singing, some even yelling at the game's referee, a distinct presence certainly didn't fit in the picture. Right across from me, just as squeezed between other people at the bar as I was, sat a young man crying.

I stared for a few seconds that felt like an hour, then, dragged back by my ever-late self consciousness, I whipped my gaze over my gin and tonic, head down, guilty for disrupting another persons's fragile moment, even if just with my eyes. It was confusing, and a bit shocking, a bit frightening that first moment, like when I first saw a deer in our backyard, late in the evening, the sun not really helping me distinguish the gentle creature from the thrilling creations of my city raised mind. After a bad actor's sip from that short glass I looked again, this time with a clearer head (first time some gin would do that to anyone) and motivated also by the thought that he might have stopped. For how long can a man cry? Surely some fast tears made him feel better, biologically taming those feelings. But how the river of my wrongful assumptions flew… the young man was still crying. Again, guilty for belittling someone else's feelings or their power to deal with them. He wasn't making a big fuss about it though, no sobbing, no sounds, only the never ending tears and the occasional tight closing of his eyes, like never wanting to open them again, but he was trying to hide it by arresting a napkin tight into his fist and using it every other moment, yet napkins get damp fast and the bunch of used ones next to his drink was quickly turning into a small white mountain. I soon saw that that couldn't have happened, because the old bartender lady was clearing them as soon as they got a bit too many. She surely noticed the young man and probably tried to help him not attract too much attention, she herself minding her work and nothing else. I guess an experienced bartender knows these things. But I don't know about other people, those other people around. They did the same thing, not minding him, not reacting, yet this seemed a bit more tragic than a bartender weighing the situation and smoothly doing her job. Some probably really didn't notice him, some surely didn't notice him as they were laughing hysterically with their peers and I refuse to believe such lack of empathy exists even in the most awful person, some might have pretended (like me) not to notice him yet they thought it might be better to leave him alone for his sake. Some maybe for their own sake. He didn't know it anyhow, avoiding eye contact with anyone except the bartenders, probably not eager to find confusion or pity in their eyes. It didn't matter, no-one did anything about this young man. This lovely airport Irish pub ran smoothly probably just like any other day. From where I was sitting it was an awfully dynamic painting except for its subject, positioned slightly to the right, yet a mile closer to the center than he'd probably wished. The perfect seat can be hard to come by.

He was drinking an old fashioned, no ice. At least that's what he ordered, for I never saw him drink it. He was just holding his hand around it when he wasn't busy wiping his tears. The lady next to him got up and while gathering her bags, she dropped something. To my surprise, the young man jumped right off his seat, helped her with a box she dropped and even offered a smile to her gratitude. Whatever he was crying about, it wasn't crushing his manners. He got back on his seat and in this short break from his tears, he caught me looking. I didn't want to play the fool, so after a couple of seconds I raised my glass a bit and gave a subtle nod.

"Cheers, kid!" I thought.

I felt bad for the young man so I figured I should take that open seat next to him and maybe use my 55 years on this Earth to offer some wisdom. Not that I'm a wise person, but at least some insights on life. Maybe just a talk at a bar.

I left my gin and tonic there, took my bag and went round the bar towards the free bar stool, part of me hoping it would be taken by the time I'd get there.

"You mind if I sit here?"

"No, sir" making an impression right away.

"An old fashioned, please" I asked the bartender lady.

"You know, it's a shame to waste a glass of scotch" I said, not looking at him.

"Oh, this..." as he looked at his glass. "I'm not such a big drinker" he answered smiling. Surprisingly, his tears had stopped, his eyes red still.

"Maybe you just need a drinking partner. A responsible drinking partner" I joked as the bartender brought my drink.

He laughed shortly. He smiled. One of those smiles polite people fade away slowly, fighting to keep it long enough for their insecurity to look away.

"I saw it in a movie" he said. "This... cool cat was always drinking scotch. He had a lot goin' on in his life and scotch kinda seemed to fix it. Made everything work." He wasn't pretending I or people around us didn't know about his crying.

"Like Humphrey Bogart?" I asked, unsure if the kid would know that generation of actors.

"Yeah. Exactly!" He stood upright now. Some eye contact. The talk was working. "It was even set in the '50s. You know, the suits, the slick back hair, the hats and all that... yeah... and he drank scotch. Always wanted to try it. Never thought I'd need a reason though."

"Well, kid, here's to hats, suits and slick back hair!" I raised my glass and fortunately the young man did too. "Do you like it?"

"It's alright. I guess it's the type of taste you eventually grow to like."

"Well, I don't think most people drink it for its taste. Like that character of yours."

"Yeah, I know..."

I don't know how much time I spent there, watching the game, sipping that scotch, talking to the kid about random things, I even forgot about his crying. Looking back, he acted like he had forgotten too. But I do remember that moment, like a breach in time, like a tap on one's shoulder, when I turned my head towards him to comment on the game, only to see him, one foot away, defeated by the river of tears that flooded his cheeks.

IRISH BAR

It took him a moment before reaching for the stack of napkins, the only endless source, besides his tears.

"Is there something I can do to help you, kid?" I helplessly whispered.

He tried to rewind this scene, embarrassed, by accelerating his wiping, hiding the napkin in his pocket this time, stamping a smile on his still wet face, only for the arching of his mouth to fall under pressure a few seconds later. He surrendered.

"I wish you could, sir."

"Did you lose someone? I don't want to butt in, but I've been through loss and..."

And he interrupted me.

"It's not that, sir. I'm good" he said.

My eyebrows clenched. "Then what's wrong?" I thought out-loud.

"It's not... anything. I'm just sad. I don't have a good reason."

I wanted to push harder. My curiosity mostly. And, myself being raised in a different time, in a more assertive way, I did.

"Come on, kid. There's got to be something. You know... something that's bugging you. Something that's hurting."

"Not really, sir. There might have been stuff in the past, but that's over, there's nothing to it anymore. Yet, the feeling remains."

"Well... if you say there's no reason to be sad and everything is alright, then why cry?" trying to encourage him to see things differently, even though I was still confused.

"Sir, I don't know how to explain it. It's just sadness. And it is stubborn, here to stay, even if it's not invited anymore. Like hurting from a punch when no-one's hitting you. It's like a dark cloud filling up every room I'm in even if it's sunny outside. I'm not crying because of anything that would make me sad. I think I just cry because of the feeling of sadness."

Even more confused, I felt I wasn't the right person to console this young man. I felt a bit helpless. But I didn't want to burden him with my confusion and I surely didn't want to slip any sort of indirect subjective judgment of the situation he was in. If my 55 years on this Earth taught me anything is that they are too few to pretend to understand everything and everyone.

"Listen, kid... I think you should go home to your family and I'm sure they'll help you out" I said with a confident tone that I hoped would rub off on him.

"It's where I'm headed now, sir. They're picking me up at the airport" he subtly smiled, showing a sort of light at the end of the tunnel. At least I saw it.

The game was almost finished, when they announced the boarding for his flight. The young man thanked me for the company and offered me a firm hand shake. I wished him all the best in the world and he then left. I kept my seat.

My flight would have been quite soon after that, but then I heard it had been delayed for a while. I found myself ordering another old fashioned and just waiting. The game was over, so I was just looking around, enjoying the music, analyzing the bar. All the seats were always taken. Maybe this wasn't my first time on this side of the bar. But I don't remember anyone joining me for a whiskey.

HOLDING HANDS WITH THE SEA

The floor tasted like metal. Sharp and never ending through my heart. Alive and flowing across the Atlantic, waking me up with gentle swings, reminding me to never pick a fight over a girl. The punches hurt more when she cheers for the other man. Love gave me the final blow. Robbed of my ego and my faith in love, I pushed myself up to the stingy thought of seeing them together for the next four days till we reached America.

Only thing I hoped for in that moment was to peacefully reach the upper floor to get some ice from the restaurant. Or an iceberg to end my misery. That famous one from eleven years ago must still be lurking somewhere out there, in the darkness of the night.

A waitress was kind enough to provide the ice. I thought she was pretty. I would have paid more attention but for the distracting heartache. Still, the ice felt good. Like the sip of a fresh start. Something I'd truly taste soon enough in the New World. So with a bag full of ice and a beer I stole from an unsupervised tray in the restaurant, I made my way towards the front deck to linger on soon-to-be-forgotten feelings while listening to the waves and staring at the stars. God was good to me. He slapped me over the head to get my eyes off that no good woman and now offered all of this for me to recover. Cheers!

"Colin!"

Not quite the voice of God.

*

My good friend, Freddy, although a devoted friend since our junior years, was a bit late to the dance. Counting on him didn't do my bones any good, but at least I got to see the true face of that sly miss. He never liked her, so maybe he missed the fight on purpose. It would be quite a rough way to teach someone the laws of attraction.

"I came as soon as I heard. You hurt?"

"I'm fine. It's my pride that took the hardest hit."

"She... uhm... still around?" he clumsily packaged the lie in an attempt to pamper my ego.

"Nah... went with that other fella. They're probably celebrating the victory by making out somewhere on the baggage floor."

"Is that what you had planned after that unlikely triumph?" He couldn't keep serious. We both started laughing.

"Gimme some o' that beer" snatching my beer the same way I snatched it from that tray earlier.

"I sure as hell told ya about that broad. Never trust a girl with that much red lipstick on. Burns your soul and she won't even look at the ashes..."

"Alright. I think I got it after all those punches. Gimme that beer back."

"You need to find someone like my sweet Frances."

"Is that the fat lady from yesterday's lunch? Did you hook up with her? Don't tell me that's why you missed the fight!"

"Hey don't talk trash about my girl." His head then turned towards the ocean, his gaze getting lost across the uptight waves, like trying to find the horizon in the middle of the night, like looking for the edge of the sea. The guy was in love. "She's a real cutie pie."

"More like a wedding cake, if you ask me," I concluded.

"Shut up!" he punched me in the shoulder, laughing.

I laughed too. I was happy for my friend. Until not even half an hour before I felt the same way about some girl. Maybe his feelings would last longer.

*

We tried to keep that beer going for as long as we could. Sharing it didn't help, but it's better to drink half a beer with a friend than a full one alone. Especially after that night's conclusion. However, just as some laugh about their past love failings, other start living theirs. Freddy was fired up on his jokes and the girl, the fight, the fake love, they all just seemed like a bad dream from long ago. Still, my attention was subtly falling for an increasingly agitated quarrel between a man and a woman on the upper deck behind us. Not even the aroused waves in the dead of the night could blur a couple's fight. I guess we all get there from time to time.

"Lookin' for drama again?" Freddy asked, looking at me with a straight face.

I hoped I wasn't, but right as I turned my head toward the ocean again in an attempt to mind my own business, I picked on a harsh sound of metal on metal. It seemed they dropped something. I wanted to help.

"What now?" my annoyed friend complained. He tried to get a last sip out of that empty bottle, then threw it in the ocean; no message inside, just some cuss words as he followed me.

The ship's tired lamps sure seemed a lot more powerful in this shinny object. Found it right away. I could feel those punches all over again as I crouched to pick it up, but it was worth it. It was the most beautiful piece of jewelry I had ever seen. A sterling locket necklace, the shape of a perfect sphere, untouched by the roughness of time passing, with not even a scratch from its fall, so clear and smooth like it was just passed on to me by the careful hands of its polisher.

"Hey! You dropped something!" I yelled as I stood up.

"Open the goddam thing!" Freddy's voice commanded over my shoulder. A gentle click and it revealed its true beauty. An engraved heart overlooking the photo of a young elegant lady. Who would've hoped for such a dazzling sight in the middle of a dim ocean? Especially in my unworthy hands.

I kept it. And that night, in my wobbly upper bunk bed, I stared at it till I fell asleep. Freddy tried to convince me to trade it at a pawn shop once we reached America. It would've brought a nice financial aid for my new start there. Also, he knew I would've shared with great joy some of the money with my childhood friend. But somehow, parting ways with this necklace didn't seem right. I wasn't going to wear it, but keeping it in my pocket felt just as glorious, like a vacation house somewhere in the Scottish highlands that no-one knows about. One can dream.

*

Next day tasted bitter sweet. I hung around our crowded deck for the few hours the likes of us were allowed, slipping between the enthusiasm of new opportunities awaiting in America and the blues of yesterday. The games kept us entertained, as everyday. I wouldn't really participate, but I enjoyed watching other people compete in our very own floating "olympic games". Most popular one was the so called "Novelty Pillow Fight". Two persons would sit on a slippery spar and try to knock each other down with a pillow. They used a few layers of blankets as a cushion for the fall, except for the ones trying to win a bet. They'd make it riskier by falling straight on the hard wooden floor. More entertainment for us, I guess. Freddy was quite good at it and people would cheer to his stubbornness of sticking to that wooden horizontal pole. "King of the Pillows" they would shout. He tried to convince me to bet on him. Always with the business ideas. Again I'd refuse.

But that one day, amidst the laughter and the pillow feathers, I noticed a presence unfit for our lower class deck. Two beautiful girls dressed with clothes made of fabrics clearly too expensive to belong to this crowd. They were both dazzling, but one was special. One was the girl from the photograph.

"Excuse me, miss!" I overconfidently approached her. "Are you lost?"

"We're quite alright, thank you!" her friend protectively intervened, trying to dismiss me. "Come on, Linda!"

"I don't mean to bother you, but I think I have something that belongs to you" I insisted as they tried to make their way through the crowd.

"What do you mean?" Linda asked while her friend tried to push her forward.

I pulled the necklace out of my pocket and waved it through the salty air. She looked intrigued and came back, against her friend's will. "What's this?"

She now looked confused, which also confused me.

"It's you. The photograph inside" I tried to explain.

I gave it to her and she gently opened it. Her big beautiful blue eyes opened up even more in surprise. She showed it to her friend. They whispered words upon words.

"Where did you get this?" her accusatory friend asked.

"I found it on the floor last night."- looking at Linda - "You know… the quarrel… I was there with my friend. I shouted at you, but…"

"This isn't me!" she interrupted my story.

"What do you mean it isn't you?"

"It isn't. I think it's my grandmother."

"Oooh… I see. Well, close enough" and I foolishly smiled.

Things were complicated, but I didn't think too much about that. The moment was overwhelming for me, talking to this out of my league girl and dodging her friend's innuendos at the same time. Rescue was on the way.

"Well Hello there!" Freddy butted in. "What did I miss?"

A few minutes and he took the friend out of my hair as Linda tried to make some sense out of the situation. Soon we ended up talking about everything. She told me about her family. She was a free spirit, thus the exploration, against her friend's will, of our lower, far from glamorous deck. She heard about our silly games and wanted to experience them, being bored with the dull activities of the first class. At some point the fancy food looses its taste and the silverware looses its shine.

*

"You know, she's here, with us, on this ship" she said.

"Who's here?"

"My grandmother. The one in the photograph."

"I thought you said you'll return the necklace to her. I thought you meant back home in the States."

"I did. But after the games finish. They're too much fun to miss" she smiled with a warmth no upper class person ever showed me.
"In fact, maybe you can give it to her yourself."

"Are you serious? You think that's alright?"

"Yes. I'm sure she'll appreciate it."

We made our way towards a big reception, where she knew her grandmother would be. It was the four of us, but somewhere along the way, Freddy and Linda's friend, got lost. Could have gotten inspired by my baggage floor plan.

"Nana."

Her grandmother, an old but very stylish lady, lifted her head from a book she was enjoying, then sunk her reading glasses to the tip of her nose to look at us, only to reveal the same beautiful blue eyes that her granddaughter had. Those blue eyes in the photograph.

"Oh, there she is! I see you've made new friends."

"Nana, this is Colin. He's got something for you."

"Well, what would a fine young man like yourself have to offer an old fogey like me?" she said smiling.

*

I liked her warm attitude. I could see that Linda got much more than just the eyes from her grandmother. Sweet charisma gliding through generations. But things changed once I pulled out the necklace from my scraggy coat. Her face turned to stone and I thought I'd lost her smile forever. I felt guilty somehow so I started explaining. I didn't steal it. I found it. I wasn't going to sell it, like my friend Freddy suggested. I took care of it. I returned it.

She took it from my hand, slid her glasses up her nose and opened the locket. Tears flooded her eyes and soon started wetting the book on her lap. But this story was better than the one in the book.

"This is from another life" she said, her voice trembling.

But the couple, the quarrel, the upper deck, the broken chain, the luck I had to hear it drop and find it and take it and return it…

"Oh, we did fight…"

"Who did you fight with, nana?" Linda asked, worried about her grandmother.

"Your grandfather. Back then. It was right where Paul said. On this same ship."

Linda was just as confused as I was.

"In 1887. It was our first time returning to Ireland in 19 years after we moved to America. We were excited about seeing our relatives and hometown again, something most immigrants can only dream of. We had some luck. The sort of luck your grandfather harnessed with his bare hands. It brought more than food on the table. It brought us, your parents and you the financial privilege we like to enjoy. Of course, he couldn't have done it without my moral support."

She winked at me and offered us the most mischievous smile I've ever seen on an old lady. We smiled as well, hoping her tears were long gone.

"Yet a sort of remorseful sensitivity coated us. I don't know… we imagined how our lives could've turned differently if we hadn't left. How this everyday longing for home wouldn't tap on our shoulders so hard. That trip caught our feelings by surprise. But we wouldn't talk about it openly.

Just a few words about how the ship seems to swim faster towards Ireland. I used to say that when we watched the back of the ship in the morning. Then some evenings he'd say he felt his Irish accent was decaying, which was nothing short of the most ridiculous idea I had ever heard, since only an Irish person could really understand what he was saying half the time" she laughed on these last words.

"And then, one night, I guess it all came raining down on us. It's what you get if you're not honest and open to each other at the right time. You better get that into your young heads! After dinner, he was feeling quite agitated, so he excused himself and went outside for some fresh air. A few minutes passed, so I followed him to this upper deck to see if he's alright. His black suit blended in with the open dark. I went next to him and didn't really say anything. But there was no need, because he started murmuring straight away. Like he couldn't hold the angst in him anymore. Or maybe, I don't know... maybe he was just afraid he'd lose the courage to let it all out. So he started babbling for some minutes about how we sold our souls for money, how he served our vanity by creating those jewelries, how we left our families behind for personal gain. He would've probably continued with the non-sense but for my slap."

Linda gasped. She was really into the story. I guess she didn't know much about her grandparents' life.

"You know how I get" her grandmother continued. "I don't deal well with hogwash. I'm a down to earth human being. I've always been this way and I'm proud of it. I missed Ireland too, but we had our own family now. It was him, myself, your mother and your uncle. And God would've sure struck us down if your grandfather kept on cursing his gift for us, our good fortune. So after I slapped him, I reached into his shirt and pulled out a locket necklace he made and always wore. I told him if he can't appreciate what that necklace stood for, then someone else should. I let him have a good look at it and then snapped it off his neck and threw it away. I walked back inside the restaurant."

"What happened afterwards?" Linda and myself synced.

"We got on with our lives. We never talked about it again, but I think he got the message. Ireland was nice. But it wasn't home anymore. And, luckily, he saw that."

*

"I think the slap helped" Freddy added.

"It probably did." We both burst into laughter.

"So how did the old lady explain the situation? How on Earth did you find the necklace after all these decades?"

"She said something about how, in the end, the necklace finally got found by someone who would be worthy of those precious values she mentioned."

"And what do you think?" he slyly threw this question at me. I didn't know if my friend was actually curious or he was just messing with me.

"I think it's a pretty tale. One of those old people anecdotes, the type they like to use as a lesson to younger folk. I'm just happy I met Linda along the way."

But I didn't really know what I thought. The look in her eyes as she told that story. She was looking back at that trip, seeing every move, hearing every sorrowful sentence again. Those were the same tears as back then, I'm sure.

"What about Linda's friend, Jenna? Did you guys hook up?"

"What? No, mate. We just talked. She's a fine gal, but I told you, I already got a girl. My sweet Frances."

It was becoming clear now. The old lady's story was fake. If it were true, the necklace would've found its way into Freddy's hands.

RED LIGHT

All three of them knew Tony, the bouncer. They were regulars, but only Damien stopped to ask him how he was.

"Alright, see ya later, man!" Damien said as he lifted his arm for a fist bump. His pals were just regulars. Damien was a friend.

He followed the dark corridor towards the bar, the voices of people having fun getting louder with every step. Three bottles of beer awaited on the counter next to his friends; one without alcohol because he was driving that night and his friends knew better than to challenge his principles.

"So, are you racing next week, Damien?" one of his friends asked as he took a first sip of his beer.

"Naa, they're rescheduling the end of the season. They don't want our rallies to mix with some local event. Logistics… We'll probably race on Christmas day or something" Damien joked.

"Well, that'd be quite a hell of a present for you, I'm sure."

They all laughed and they cheered for his potential victory. The non-alcoholic beer tasted just fine.

Damien loved this place. The music, the atmosphere, the girls, the red brick walls carrying those oversized wooden frames with a small photo inside each of them of the same long gone owner, some Irish immigrant who married his bar. Well, he didn't love it as much as that fella. Still, it was more than his comfort zone. It was the place one hopes to reach after leaving his comfort zone.

*

Second round of beers on the way, thirst building up, all three of them laughing desperately about some resurfaced high school memory, when he saw her. The vintage light bulbs grazed her beautiful brown hair. The rest of her glowed on its own. He couldn't have missed her. Nobody did. But in spite of the lack of alcohol in that beer, he left his friends and confidently got up and went to say "Hi!". His friends excitedly watched him go, but were interrupted by the bartender as he pushed the sweating beer bottles towards them. A joyous "Cheers" and looking again at their friend and his evening crush already seemed like a different movie. Smiles and warm physical chemistry that made everyone around jealous.

"And right after that I found my friends in the crowd. Or they found me, to be honest…" Mia served Damien her precious memories like she had known him forever. It had only been 10 minutes, but the chemistry was right on time.

"Well, I'm sure you can find your way around the dance floor" Damien said as he bent a slick smile.

It was a nice place. And people danced here. And although they both enjoyed their bonding conversation, they knew better than to waste a Saturday not dancing. She smiled back and poshly, but in a goofy way, lifted her hand to be led towards the dance floor. Damien didn't shy away, grabbed her hand and they went straight to the center of the dance floor, only to be met by the loud gawky cheers and whistles of his, by now, tipsy friends. Mia found it funny and cute, especially because Damien, contrary to his straight forward attitude, blushed. The dance went on.

*

By the third song they started whispering so many things in each other's ear that the dance didn't really matter anymore. It was unapologetically consumed, leading them to this other stage in their meeting, where they just couldn't get enough of each other.

"Do you wanna go for a drive? I heard they're setting up the lights downtown. I heard they're beautiful" Damien's words drifted away from their original meaning as he was getting lost in her eyes. But he was doing it on purpose, subtly telling her she was beautiful.

"You're not that subtle" she laughed. "But yes. I'd love to go for a drive with you."

However confident Damien was, that last sentence of hers hugged his experienced manly heart. His smile wasn't slick anymore, losing its mirror perfected one sided curve and applying the original muscle memory of his face, a more honest, vulnerable smile making way.

They split ways, their holding hands understanding this a bit late, to get their coats and say goodbye to their friends, agreeing to meet up front. Damien's friends didn't say much, they just nodded their heads in a funny, sarcastic way and lifted their beers in his honor. Guy stuff.

*

"Already leaving?" a concerned Tony asked as Damien's silhouette approached him from the dark corridor. As his face was revealed by the entrance light spots, Damien's smile explained everything. "You are. But not alone." These words synchronized with his lifting arm for another of their trademark fist bumps, followed by a proud chuckle. "Blonde or brunette?"

"More like that Irish whiskey the owner used to worship" Damien's gaze piercing upwards into the air.

"Kinda stingy that breed of alcohol. You keep that in mind" Tony pushed those words with a fatherly care, something Damien appreciated.

That same minute, Mia showed up, and after a quick introduction of Tony and a polite hand shake, the two disappeared into the parking lot across the street, their laughter dissipating between nagging car horns.

His car, his sanctuary, his taming of the vast wild concrete underneath them, the spinning rubber taking its time kissing it across its main roads. They were cruising, enjoying the beautiful lights Damien mentioned, rarely saying a word to let the bass of a Tiesto song mix with the cool urban background, taking pleasure in the simple presence of the other. He met a distant feeling of guilt, as he always played this song on a first drive with a new girl (he had a special playlist which he considered to be the perfect soundtrack for such occasions), yet he liked her more than other girls. He thought she deserved more than an overshared playlist.

"Just this song" he thought. Then he turned the volume down a bit and let the car's exhaust system do the singing. Words, laughter and more bonding followed.

*

The lights suddenly turned to red, so they stopped. Surprising position for a couple so young, so incapable of standing still, so eager to move fast, especially with 300 untamed horses under the hood. But when the young stop, they don't waste time or energy. They laugh, windows open, they're not ashamed. The night is theirs and they can do whatever they want, even though every once in a while a red light meets them and they obey. Damien's joke-telling was on fire. Mia's cheeky sense of humor built on it. His hand was out the window, the other one grabbing firmly the upper part of the wheel. His body language spoke cocky and relaxed at the same time. Mia was leaning towards him like the space between them was too much.

It was summer and the weather could have been described as missing, but his hand by the window suddenly felt a light breeze. A van pulled to their side. Damien slowly, uninterested and frankly by mistake,

looked at the driver. He exchanged a few seconds with the man's eyes then green light hit and he and his date were long gone. Only the smell of burned rubber and a fading echo of their youthful laughter remained. The man's old van slowly started to move as well.

*

He turned right. He had no business with the youngsters, other than sharing a summer's night red light with them. However, he was a bit judgmental. A bit angry at their generation. A bit jealous of their youth. A bit hurt by life's way of shuffling privilege.

"Spoiled rich kids." He didn't refrain from labeling them right there, in that neutral gear box position, and saying it too. Not out loud, but definitely through that eye contact. The nasty Saturday work day he was leaving behind didn't help. But now it was almost over. A few more red lights and the comfort of his home would balance everything out.

He parked Joanna, his nicknamed van, in front of his house like he always did: right side on the sidewalk, driver's side on the road. A neighbor who's also a mechanic once told him that this asymmetrical way of parking would one day soon damage the car's suspensions. He didn't want that to happen to Joanna. And more importantly the car was his job, his way of putting food on the table for his family. But the road was too narrow and the sidewalk as well. Blocking either of them was out of the question since he worked mostly during the night so the car would be parked there during daytime, causing distress for others when they needed their road and sidewalk most. He ran on hope and trust. His Joanna's suspensions would last.

Zzz

*

The chicken in the front yard were making some noises as he entered.

"You're supposed to start chitchatting at sunrise" he tiredly commented. The thought of organizing a big chicken dinner for his family and friends crossed his mind. "It would make some nice room for Joanna" he assumed. But his tiny front yard could barely fit half of the van. And he would never get rid of his chicken. His father was a farmer and once upon a time it was his dream too. But the expansion of the city and the ever changing paths of life led him to something else. Driving wasn't so bad. A master at changing focus from the half empty to the half full glass.

The ever-present night battle with the door's creak was waiting. He always tried his best, yet always lost. But it didn't matter that much this time, because the TV was turned on to cover the noise. His son fell asleep watching it and instead of waking him up and sending him to his room, our late night driver joined him on the couch. A rerun of the football game was on and luckily he didn't know the final score. The game, the soft couch after so many hours on that evil driver's seat, his son next to him; everything really was balanced now. And it wasn't just any game. The son of a famous footballer he always admired had already scored. It made him happy. Hearing the commentator praise the same name as 20 years before, seeing it reunite with that legendary number 10 beneath it brought the joy of the old days back once more. It wasn't even his favorite team but he rooted for this kid out of a deep longing for a time when things were different for him, a sort of selfish time machine to support his melancholy. But it wasn't really about that. He rooted for him as a thank you to his father and all the wonderful exciting memories he had created. A thank you to the past. The glass was half full.

*

He didn't remember the moment he closed his eyes. He opened them now and carved sun rays filtered through an old curtain to announce him it was already morning. Quite impressed with the fact that he wasn't awaken by the conversation his wife and his son were having just next to him, he stood up, ready for some breakfast.

"How's everybody doin'?" he interrupted them.

They didn't really answer as their conversation about school was more important, but then again, he didn't really expect an answer as he passed them to get to the kitchen. He served himself some freshly made omelette and came back to the living room to enjoy it in front of the TV. It was a good day, work was far ahead and he could enjoy some simple time around his home and family.

Despite the far from ideal sleep he had, the couch felt just as soft. He sat comfortably, food on his lap on his favorite trencher and shuffled the TV channels in search of the perfect program to enjoy his breakfast. The remote controller felt like the best invention ever in these moments. But the search for that perfect program was abruptly paused by a news channel. Bad TV news has a way of making people get in their own way, even though it has nothing to do with their own personal lives. It showed a crash on TV, several people wounded and 2 dead. A sports car, young driver, rich parents. Our van driver didn't need to see that it was a different person. All he heard was last night's car tires leaving that red light. All he saw was Damien's face.

BLUE LIGHT

The blue screen light gently caresses the empty walls of the room. It's time for Denis to wake up. His body can't take this uncomfortable position anymore this late at night. Eyes half open, keyboard keys indented all over his left cheek, he lifts his pulsating head barely supported by his numb neck. The glasses never left his face, but climbed his forehead while he slept, so readjusting them was the first step for returning to work. The blue light hits his retina like a whip on sunburned skin. Glasses' protection doesn't work on a forty hour work day. He checks for the upper right corner of the screen and he still has time. Even for a Coke refill. Bones crack as he gets up from his chair. A scary, but satisfying sound, the only sound that fills this cold room besides his neurotic typing and a lazy computer vent. For a while at least, because a text message sound fades behind him while he walks undisturbed towards the kitchen.

A blue light hits Denis again in the otherwise unlit apartment, as he opens the fridge. This time he means to finish the work so he takes the bottle of Coke with him. No more kitchen breaks, even though he hoped this one would've felt a bit longer.

Back in his work room he finds the courage to start again. A few stretches and deep breaths and he claims the chair again. He negligently refills his glass right next to his keyboard, one of those illogical risks tired people take and sometimes win. A long first sip with tiny fizzy bubbles splashing the lenses of his glasses and he restarts his brain, ready to deep dive into his work again and finish this project on time. But it is only placebo, for Coke has long lost its power over Denis and his irresponsible work ethic. He first did it for the effect, now only the action remains. Talk about the power of habit.

The typing starts again. The clicking accompanies. The pen is a victim of fidgeting. The papers around his laptop shuffle often enough to mistake them for a deck of oversized playing cards. Denis's workflow is on fire and the confidence of finishing everything by morning is gently conquering his mental state. It's these moments that sustain his will of getting involved in projects with such short deadlines. He always gets away with it. But he can't last immersed in that productive state, not while his slick cat begs for attention, especially now, at two o'clock in the morning, after its usual race around the house. A true creature of the night. Just like Denis.

His fascination for such animals far outranks his dedication to his work, so he stops for a second to pet it, simultaneously feeding himself the excuse that he's got plenty of time at the rate he's working. He chuckles as the cat methodically circles his chair back and forth and starts wondering why he didn't get a pet earlier in his life. Was it because he didn't have enough time for a pet? A dog might need walking twice a day, but a cat doesn't need much.

"Still, maybe it needs another cat for companionship..." he thinks. He seriously considers getting a second cat for a few seconds before he abruptly, and without any conclusion, abandons the idea. Did he not get a pet because of that dog that bit him when he was a kid? Or because of his neighbor's aggressive cat? None of these things ever crossed his mind before, but it didn't matter anymore. Some things just end up alright. His cat was long part of the family, someone who was always there for him.

That ultimate balance point on his squeaky plastic chair, the one he always pursued to the limit as he'd lean on the backrest risking a not-so-gracious fall, it never seemed as comfortable as now, so perfectly attuned to his control, so ideal for his stretching position, so empowering to his working ego. Quick enough to grab his desk and prevent falling on his back, he actually shakes his desk and spills some Coke on his work. If at any point in these intense two seconds Denis intuitively wanted to be silent and mislead the late night visitor into thinking no-one was home. The plan is now unequivocally crushed by his loud and angered shouting and cursing as he chaotically looks for paper towels to stop the Coke from ruining his work. He can't find any. His t-shirt will have to do.

Although not as intense as the previous minute, the cursing doesn't stop as Denis makes his way towards the door. What is more, the doorbell situation only adds to his frustration, somewhat blaming the unknown visitor for the spill. But despite his curiosity, he guesses that it might be his brother, Alex, whom he had an argument with the previous day. They don't see each other much, but every once in a while, Alex, as he is a sort of a night owl himself, drops by unannounced and uninvited after clubbing. Denis is right.

He opens the door, but stands dead center as to suggest a quick interaction before closing the door with each brother on a different side.

"Hey man! Did I wake you up? Can I come in?" Alex respectfully asks. The supposed arrogance and ignorance of the previous day is gone, leaving Denis with no leverage for an easy dismissal. His ego jumps in and suggests Alex might be here for an apology, a cheap hint at what he truly wishes. With that in mind, Denis moves to the side, inviting Alex in and taking pride and comfort in being part of this hypothetical reconciliation. Still his pride is complex.

"Sure. But I've got some work to finish so..." Denis says.

"Yeah man. Don't worry. I'll be out of your hair in a bit" Alex assures him as he strongly pats him on his shirtless back, then passes him and goes straight for the living room.

Was it just acting? Just some smooth innocent questions to grease himself into Denis's home? Denis instantly regrets this decision of letting him in and not being more assertive in this late night interaction, especially after their stupid argument.

He locks the door and surrenders his upper body to a deep sigh, the kind of sigh that struggles to replace a good cigarette. Following his brothers' annoying humming, an ever-present side effect to his tipsy condition, he enters the dark living room to find Alex already sitting in his armchair, the only piece of comfortable furniture in his whole apartment.

A silent brotherly agreement for not turning the light on is set. The hallway light slashing through the living-room's carpet should be enough. Denis leans on his heater and crosses his skinny arms, partly because at this point he relies on body language to send his brother off, but mostly because he doesn't have another chair anywhere near and he's getting a bit cold without any t-shirt on.

"You've been working out? Were you doin' push-ups just now?" Alex asks ironically.

"Definitely."

"What's up with all these boxes, man? When are you getting some real furniture?" Alex continues with the irony.

"I'm failing to understand how that is any of your concern" Denis smugly replies.

"Hey man. I'm just asking. Just tryin' to be a good bro."

A few seconds pass and Denis's refusal to contribute to the conversation obliges Alex to go on talking.

"Club 27 was awesome tonight, man. It was just incredible. You should've seen the girls. I'm telling you, you should come sometimes, hang around. You could use a drink. Mix some of that Cola of yours with some real liquor. A change of scenery might be good for you."

"I'm doin' great as is, don't worry" Denis bitterly responds.

"Suit yourself, man. But I'm telling you, there are things in life that you don't really wanna do, until you do them. Then you regret not doing it earlier. You really regret it. Come to think about it, it's kind of a paradox. Cause if you try it now, you'll absolutely regret that you haven't done it all this time. So you're better off not doing it."

The alcohol was surely racing through Alex's bloodstream at this point.

"I go to bars with my friends all the time, man" Denis impatiently canceled any other attempt at continuing that monologue.

"You do? Well… I guess I don't know you that well. I'm sure your friends do. I'm sorry I'm not one of them. I'd better go and let you finish your work."

Alex stands up and walks with a perfect balance towards the door. All his remaining focus probably went into that walk. Denis follows him.

"Good night, man…" Alex says while walking towards the elevator.

Denis waits for a few seconds for the hallway light sensor to react and take care of his drunk brother from that point on. His patience is long beaten by frustration, so anticipating the moment, he closes and locks the door just as the light comes on. He leans with his cold skinny arms on the door, like pushing it to never open again, and looks at the floor, judging himself for not being more assertive, blaming his brother for unfitting arrogance, if arrogance can take such forms, questioning himself for blaming his brother, unsure of his own behavior in this upsetting brotherly rapport, regretting such a strong need for his brother's apology. There's never time for things that matter, there's never time for family, because work awaits. Denis skips this thoughtful state and confidently walks back to his so called work room, trying to autosuggest how much he actually cares about family affairs. He digs through his Coke flavored papers to try and re-immerse himself into work, but it's challenging, just as he feared it would be. The tiredness, the mess on his desk, the unexpected lack of dark soda, the doorbell that caused most of it.

"He didn't even mention the fight" his mind fumes.

It is late. Going on like this can't possibly be a way to finish work. He calms himself down and slowly but surely returns to work. About half an hour passes and he stops to massage his temples and forehead. He needs a short one minute break to recalibrate his concentration. Normally he would have a sip of sugary caffeine, but in this situation he reaches for his phone, another source of eye-whipping blue light that would normally cancel the benefits of that massage, however the screen stirs his mind and reminds him that he received a message a few hours back.

"I'm sorry we fought yesterday. You get annoying sometimes, but I shouldn't take advantage of that and react the way I did. I'm sorry. Anyway, I'm heading to see you. Hope you're awake. I know you always are" the message read.

A fool. A regretful fool. Still, his pride overwhelms the reality of the situation and after a minute or so of feeling shame, he feels good about winning the argument, he feels good about himself. A message back in the morning should be enough to balance out his dismissive attitude regarding his brother's visit.

Work slid gracefully out of his now harmonious mind and soon translated into a reliable and timely finalized project. Another victory for late night last minute project management, even with an empty bottle of Coke and with at least two hours of sleep left before having to submit his work in person. He doesn't remember feeling so good lately, so intuitively and in spite of his tired state, he wants to enjoy it fully, but for some reason he can't. The cat jumps on the desk and meows in what might be called a call to celebration. Denis smiles and pets the cat, but he struggles remembering its name. He then suddenly feels a warm glow on his right cheek, the type of warmth a blue light can't offer, accompanied by a song by "The Killers". He knows this song, it's one of his favorites. The type of song he'd listen to while riding his bicycle to work, or maybe he'd use it in a workout playlist. But he doesn't really workout. Maybe he'd use it for his morning alarm.

Eyes half open, keyboard keys indented all over his left cheek, he realizes he's looking at the sun through his dirty window. His breath is cut short and transformed into a loud gasp that might frighten any cat, but luckily there isn't any. Several aggressive taps on the phone's screen try to shut down the alarm clock before hurrying to verify at what point during the project did he fall asleep. Too far behind, with not even enough time to make up an excuse for his superior. Nonetheless, he grabs his phone to call a person that would soon be waiting for him in his office, his trust about to be shattered. One unread message awaits him, received at that moment when he left for the kitchen, yet not from his brother.

"Change of plans: the client won't arrive until Friday, so don't bring the project tomorrow."

BIG MOUNTAINS

I remember that song. Mountains slowly rising at the edge of the world. Sticking my face to the window seemed a good idea to see them better, to get closer to them, no matter what speed my dad was driving at. Still hadn't gotten used to those automatic windows, so I'd sometimes accidentally press the button with my skinny elbow and let all that wind yell at us. I'd close it right away, not wanting a different yell from my dad. But he wouldn't mind. In spite of his preference for a peaceful drive, proper for sparking conversations undisturbed by noises such as the car's aerodynamic being broken by an open window… he liked this song.

Sitting at that kitchen table, watching my mum standing next to the stove, waiting for the food to heat, I wondered if she also remembered this song, if it meant anything to her. By the lost look on her face, she didn't and it didn't. Maybe it was the small kitchen radio that didn't really have good speakers or good reception. Most of the song was lost to static anyway. Or the closing storm outside becoming less shy with each passing minute. Maybe she was thinking about that and wasn't paying attention to the song. A wild storm could've easily torn apart her garden. Not much she could do at that point, I thought. Yet being stoic was never her thing. Maybe she did remember the song, but different feelings might have been attached to it. Feelings unlike mountains and the joy of childhood. Feelings of sadness, of regret, of things a six year old couldn't have seen. The mountains were too big and his eyes were glued to a window anyway.

"Do you want two or three pieces of chicken?" she asked, looking for my eyes as I delayed my answer.

"Two is enough" I eventually answered, knowing full well she's going to serve me three pieces.

She got married young. They got married young. Nineteen, I heard. Family didn't offer much. Town didn't offer much. Seemed the way to go. And then your 20s hit you with just how fast and sudden youth can be, so he left. Said he'll be back sooner than later, but no matter when he would have returned, that one minute conversation with his packed bag by his side molded her heart in shapes that could never fit anywhere. Not that she had high hopes for her future. She didn't have any hopes, other than building together a nice, respectful family, which seemed to her more noble than anything her favorite teacher preached about dreams and fulfillment. But at twenty one, alone yet still married she was, for divorce never really made its way into that short conversation, trapped in her hometown by a fight between feelings too contrasting to understand, she got a job at the local bakery. She liked to knit the pretzels. Reminded her of those art classes she enjoyed so much in school. That teacher wasn't her favorite for nothing, but when she dropped by to buy bread, you could see in her eyes that knitting pretzels was not what she meant when talking about the individual's expression in this world. Mrs. Donald was her name. My grandma said she always laughed at that name, said it reminded her of some cartoon, and that my mum would always jump to defend her teacher's name. My grandma never understood what good it was to inspire if you'd only help one's boss by buying bread.

"You want bread with the chicken?" she asked.

"No, thank you" I answered.

"It's fresh. I just bought it before you arrived."

My mother did mention her boss one time, the old lady who owned the bakery. On our way to grandma's house, we'd pass a big, lovely orchard filled with apple trees holding all the apples in the world. She said that, back then, her boss lived there, in a house hidden by all those apples and that she'd give them, the employees, each an apple a day. Something about keeping them healthy. From my mother's tone, she didn't care much about the old lady. She probably just had too many apples in her yard and enjoyed saying a rhyme each day.

"Do you want more chicken?"

"I'm good. Thank, you."

“How about desert after? Some fruit? Helps with digestion.”

I knew that. I’ve been told that with each home cooked meal since I was a little boy. And with all of today’s variety in a supermarket, I’d rarely get apricots, or pears, or oranges. Not that I’d demand anything different than apples.

Back then her town (and his hometown) was even smaller and less cluttered with auto workshops or hardware stores. The dirt road on the outskirts, by the water tower where my parents used to spend time as teenagers, turned at some point into a multi lane exit for a new highway and the water tower was in the way. For the ones that never walked the dirt road and never kissed under the water tower, it was progress. Others learned how ruthless progress can be.

With no one to kiss under the water tower, she still headed out there every once in a while after work to see the sunset. She’d carefully climb on the rusty ladder to reach the perfect height and angle for a splendid view, the sun falling over the thick forest just at the edge of the plains. Many years later, I could still see the forest from my backseat window as we left town each holiday. Progress hadn’t reached it. But I heard that, back then, there was more to it. There was this silence, undisturbed by cars and the future. It was probably what she went there for.

At least at first it was. The quiet. The feelings that lingered in each sunset. The memories. The hope that he’d return that exact evening, on that old dirt road guided by the last rays of the day. But my grandma says she knows this story all too well. She says that one evening, as the sun was setting, out in the field near the forest, my mother saw something else. It felt like hope, but it was just a deer. Pretty young and small, my grandma confidently claims. They would sometimes show up in the field, coming out of that forest, but this one just stood there and then sat down. And my mother saw everything and felt something was wrong. Timid steps through the dusty plains and they finally were face to face, each one more frightened than the other. The young deer didn’t seem injured. “Not on the outside at least” my mother could have thought. She had her apple with her, so she thought it would serve the deer well. An eaten apple later, the deer stood up and vividly ran back into the forest. And my mother back home.

"You haven't eaten your apple" my mother worried.

"I don't feel like eating it now. I'll save it for later" I responded.

"Well, there's a full basket in the pantry, if you later want more." Sooner than later, there she was again. Up that water tower, watching the sun rays hit the dirt road, hoping. Yet this time, every other minute, she'd also look at the edge of the forest in search of that one deer. She didn't expect much, her eyes didn't linger on that forest like they did on the damn empty dirt road. But the deer did come back. And it waited for her to get down that giant metal tree and it let her get close enough for a weak apple throw to reach it. She wouldn't have crossed a certain line and risk losing its trust anyway. Not that day at least, for the next few days the deer got close enough to eat the apple out of her hand. She couldn't help but smile. One of those rare instances when happiness sparks art.

Old Mr. Cassano's art shop would close early, not because he was getting old and didn't have any employees, but apparently the few customers that he had would always drop by in the morning to get their supplies. In reality they'd drop by in the morning because he always served his customers an espresso and they just enjoyed a quick chat over a quick italian coffee. No one needs so many pencils and erasers. So one day, my mother skipped her lunch break to get to that coffee place disguised as a graphic tools shop. She was in a hurry, she ran, as my grandma again pictures it, even though one could never arrive late anywhere in this small town. Mrs. Donald was already there, drinking her espresso, holding a bag with her still warm bread, having a chat with old Mr. Cassano over postmodernism in paintings, when my mother entered the shop with her baker's uniform still on. A truly postmodern painting, one might argue. The pretzel artist bought what she needed, enjoyed a delicious espresso rather quickly and off she was back to work. That evening she left a cloth bag with thick paper, some pencils and an apple at the bottom of the water tower, as she climbed up top to watch the road and the forest. The road didn't answer back, but the deer did and walking on her soon-to-be beaten track through the fields, she went to feed him and draw him. The deer would eat the apple and stay for a little longer, enough for her to sketch his features in pencil. She'd work on her sketches back home, adding water and colours, until they'd become paintings. They got better each week

and soon she had a full stack of them underneath her bed. She wouldn't share this with anyone, but my grandma found them and told my mother to talk to Mrs. Donald for some help with an exhibit of sorts. My mother was in a hurry, but she stopped right as she grabbed the door handle to leave the house, trying to keep her smile from showing hope and enthusiasm. She said she'll think about it, maybe after she practices a bit more.

"Oh my, the storm is really closing in..." she worried.

"I'll go and make sure all the windows are closed" I tried to assure her.

"I'm mostly worried about the vegetable garden. It might get ruined... and I was kind of proud of it."

She'd go almost everyday to that water tower, treating this adventure with a bit more seriousness and getting more motivated as time passed. Now that grandma also showed faith in her work, she had a goal in mind. And a plan. She stopped Mrs. Donald for one more second as she handed her the hot bread. Asked for a meeting sometime. About paintings. Mrs. Donald, confused yet intrigued, accepted. Enthusiasm is a hard thing to fight against. The motivation it brings can make one believe she can conquer the world. From up there, where the rusted ladder takes you, it really felt possible. But the higher you go, the bigger the fall. As she gazed towards the forest, waiting for the deer to return, the once important dirt road showed a familiar figure. She never forgot her husband, but she forgot that's why she started to go to the water tower. It was all reminded in a second. She hurried down the rusted ladder and past her bag, ran towards him and they hugged. He said he was sorry and that he missed her so much and she said it doesn't matter anymore as long as he's back. And as they walked towards town, where the dirt road turns to concrete, she stopped for a second to look back. She thought she could see if the deer had come, but the forest was too far now and she was too grounded.

That night he told her about his adventures outside their small town and she told him about apples, paintings and her new friend. The next time, she took him with her and even let him feed the deer, as she quickly sketched the scene. It all seemed sweet, but soon she found out she was pregnant and he had to get a job, working when the sun set. Her doctor suggested no animals and her husband agreed. She'd still go out to the field, just not at sunset and wouldn't climb the rusted ladder anymore. She'd leave an apple around their usual spot, at the edge of the forest, she'd take a deep breath, take in the moment, then she'd head back home. The baby arrived and about the same time, they started building that highway, pushing nature a bit further. I only know this from my grandmother, for my mother never really talks about her paintings. She talks about apples, storms and her garden, but my grandmother says it's the same thing.

WORK AND OTHER LIVES

It was the second morning in a different bed. Too soft and too cozy, like one of those vacation beds, one of those formal gifts that life throws at you every once in a while along with the responsibility of enjoying it even if you crave work. One of those hotel beds that you shouldn't get too attached to. A tiny move lured Tom deeper into the mattress and as that cloud swallowed him, still dreamy, he cracked his eyes open. The ceiling was far and getting further away as he sunk more and more for what he thought could be eternity. He thought of reaching for one of those timbers that made up the house's structure, stretched across the ceiling. He hoped to escape this comfort and return to his responsibilities, but at the border between dreams and reality you act more like a drunk, not really doing anything to help your cause, so he let go. He had nothing against alcohol, in fact he actually enjoyed a glass of scotch every other evening, but in that short moment that offered all of this, to his workaholic mind, he was the worst kind of drunk: drunk on comfort. He let the bed do its magic and closed his eyes.

An eternity later only one hour had passed and this time his dreams were long gone when he opened his eyes, rested and ready to grapple with reality and logic. By his side, his wife, Ana, was still sleeping, seemingly without the guilt that tormented his subconscious. He envied her. He hoped he could one day soon learn to relax and live without thinking about work. It was the reason they had come to live here, in a small cottage house up in the hills, close to a beautiful village lucky enough to have escaped the unforgiving wrath of tourists. It was his idea. But he forgot about it in 35 years of marriage to his work, so when things started affecting his wellbeing and propagating into their entire family,

she reminded him about this old dream of his. He trusted her, so he didn't argue much about it. It was his lazy younger self that he blamed. Yet all the right reasons were there: he was getting old and although all of his co-workers appreciated his professionalism and involvement, his career had peaked long time ago. His wife half-retired a couple of years back and now only did online financial consulting for a few clients. The kids were all grown up and taking care of themselves and their own families and even mentioned wanting some countryside place to visit every once in a while with their own kids. It all made sense. Now he only had to get used to it.

After lunch they were willing to create some sort of routine, a short walk through the fields and hills around the village, getting that mid-day break that supposedly gives great people such clarity to envision what's ahead of them, to make peace with what has been and, most importantly for himself and his wife, to appreciate the present moment. There were a few narrow dirt tracks guiding the villagers around the hills, but his wife strayed so many times off of them in search of beautiful flowers that they jokingly decided, that with enough steps, they would make their own tracks. They thought of giving it a name like "The Road to Redemption" or "Highway to Hell", but couldn't really figure out if they were sinful enough. Maybe it wasn't their say, yet blowing in a dandelion, they made a promise to influence God's take on the matter. They laughed. It seemed wild to them to have so much fun after spending most of their lives behind a desk and not really enjoying life. And just like the bed's eternal comfort, all this laughing made Tom actually feel guilty. He knew that, just as well, he was at the beginning of another road, much longer, but still one with no steps ahead to guide him. Luckily, like the new track up the hills, he'd have steps beside him.

And they managed to keep it up. It was really becoming a routine, though none of them would really dare to call it that just yet. They knew it took time for new actions to deserve that title, to become true habits, and rejoicing before the finish line, they thought would endanger the process. It's how they always lived their lives and somehow what bonded them. After about three weeks, a prolonged online meeting kept Ana from her daily break, but she encouraged him to take the walk anyway, alone, and not give the grass any chance of swallowing their tracks.

“We’re here to stay and mother nature should know that” she joked.

“We’d better find some greater sin than this” Tom joked back.

And smiling and pensive he walked out the door, getting hit right away by the beautiful view and the fresh air, stimulating his mood only like mother nature could. She got the last laugh. It was mother nature that was there to stay, in their hearts and minds, and he never put up a fight about it. He was getting it. He walked, he enjoyed the view and the sounds, he watched from afar a squirrel running up a tree, he stopped to pick up some dandelions yet as he took a second to think if it’s practical to bring them home to his wife the wind offered him a quick answer and blew them away. He liked the moment anyway. He was getting it. Closing in on the village, he climbed the wooden fence of an abandoned pen to sit there and watch some cows feed freely on the grass. Passers-by, locals, greeted him and stayed for a quick chat. Some already knew them, knew his name and his wife’s name, running into them on the daily walks. Most were welcoming and indulged in a good ol’ talk. Tom appreciated them, at first mostly through the filter of simply not being city people. He never was much of a social person outside his work or family, generally not thinking much of people, but he was now changing his mind, wondering if he simply might have been blinded by his own comfort and professional goals and that he might have missed out on the beauty of social interactions even with city people. His wife’s optimism was getting to him and he started looking forward to these conversations. He still had time to make it up. He was getting it.

As the locals he met said their goodbyes and wished for more sunny days and nice chats, Tom took a deep breath and wondered how one decides just when to go home and leave all of this. Will it still be here tomorrow? Apart from responsibilities and daylight, one could spend all day in nature. Especially now, when one does not have to work. He thought of his wife and how he already missed her, or at least how he would’ve preferred to share these moments with her, just like all the other days. And maybe nature should be given the same opportunity. Of being missed. But right before getting off that fence that provided him with such a great view and a fine place to sit while conversing with the locals, a dog approached him with contagious joy. A rough collie like the famous one in the old movies of Tom's childhood.

"Where did you come from?" Tom asked as he carefully watched his steps reach the grass.

A friendly tail wag later, the dog ran towards his owner's call like forgetting all about Tom, yet leaving him with a big smile on his face. He didn't know this pair. He raised his hand as a salute to the far away owner and got one back right away. The dog picked up on the salute as well and, after a quick pat on the head and a rewarding "Good boy", ran back towards Tom. The furry creature was entitled to his back rubs and sweet talk and demanded them as soon as he leaned against Tom's legs. Tom couldn't wait to tell his wife.

"I'm sorry about him. Come 'ere boy! Leave the man alone!" the owner shouted from afar, as he climbed the hill.

Between all those face licks, Tom raised his eyes towards the man walking up the hill.

"It's alright. He's quite friendly" he shouted back. Yet, in that moment, his soul, if he ever believed he had one, seemed to shout something back at him. He knew that man, but it didn't make sense, so he let him get closer and hopefully reveal his mistake.

"He's always like this. Thankfully he doesn't go to people that can't stand dogs. I hope he didn't mistake you for someone different."

Tom did not.

A lifetime ago, before work overwhelmed him, before he even knew what pathway he would choose, he was a joyful kid making the most of his summers in the country side, where an aunt of his lived. He wasn't more social than he'd be as an adult and he didn't have many friends, but he had a cousin. Climbing trees, chasing wild chicken, throwing rocks into the river when improvised fishing wasn't working, using a pair of old binoculars to be astounded by eagles' flight or to spy on neighbors, digging holes to hide whatever toy meant more that summer only to dig it out the next year and find out that it didn't really feel like treasure anymore, carefully picking up the right branches that would lead the greatest wooden sword fights or just simply running around the hills till hearing the aunt's voice echo over the village late at night, is how Tom and his cousin spent their summers. Tom was one year younger, so he saw his

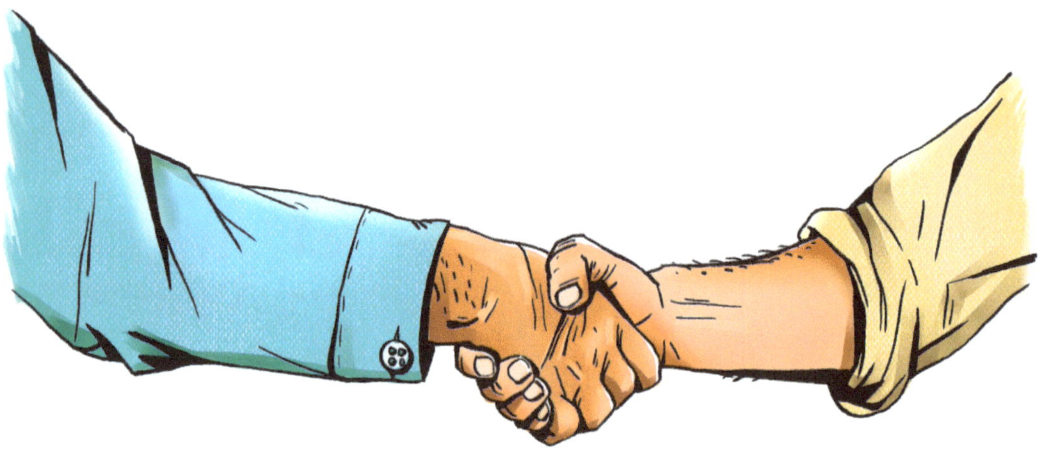

cousin as a sort of mentor, learning whatever he could from him, holding his opinions high and trusting his thoughts.

"You should always stand up straight. It'll add to your confidence and you'll also grow taller. I read it in a magazine" his cousin once said. And although Tom never reached a basketball player's size, he did always remember to stand up straight and at least understood the importance of confidence.

"You know, when you meet another man, a firm hand shake is how you show respect. We should practice so that when we grow up, we'll be ready." And they would grasp each other's hands as hard as they could until it lead to a wrestle.

Tom's parents called every week to see how he was doing and if he wanted to come back home, but he never did and his aunt always enjoyed having him over so she'd argue for his stay at the end of each phone call. At the end of each August though, before school started, his father would drive up to the hills to pick him up. Tom would hug his aunt and cousin and always ask if he could come the next summer as well. His aunt would laugh and give him another hug. Saying goodbye finished only when the distance wouldn't let him wave at them anymore from the backseat of his dad's car.

It had been what felt like a hostile amount of time before Tom realized he shouldn't keep the dog's owner with his hand stretched for that long. Still speechless, he accepted the invitation for a friendly handshake.

"Lovely out here, ain't it? Hi, I'm Matthew and this crazy fella is Bandit."

"Nice to meet you. Tom" lingering on those short letters to kickstart some sort of cosmic memory in this stranger. His cousin never reached adulthood, so he didn't really know what his face would have looked like as a 60 year old, but this gentleman surely fit the description for someone with such a firm handshake. In times like these, hope plays tricks on the mind and hooks to any little lie we tell ourselves. One suddenly gives magic or faith a chance to explain itself. His cousin's name wasn't even Matthew.

An eternity of summers too early, a week before Tom's arrival, his cousin didn't come back home. Some villagers said they'd seen him chase a dog along the river bank, others that he went for a swim around the same place. That phone call his parents received one day made Tom think all those summers were but a dream. He couldn't cry. Yet his scars from all those adventures never let him forget that dream.

Matthew told him about great places to hike to around those hills and beyond. Some fantastic tracks that lead to beautiful views. Inside the forest and under the big sky. How wonderfully coloured the squirrels that mocked his Bandit were and which mushrooms were safe to cook. How his grandkids love this place, but run too fast for his old legs. Tom enjoyed the conversation and didn't want the striking resemblance or at least his imagination take anything away from Matthew's wonderful life. But he could see a different life, a life in which his cousin returned home that day and would eventually grow old in the heart of the hills, with a big family that ate wild mushrooms and a dog that chased mischievous squirrels.

"You don't have to stay here for long to get it."

"To get what?" Tom asked.

"Life. Life, my friend."

Tom was getting it.

CPSIA information can be obtained
at www.ICGtesting.com
Printed in the USA
LVHW010728150623
749844LV00006B/19